Joseph Richard Bradway

A Beautiful Poetic Review and Friendly Offering

Joseph Richard Bradway

A Beautiful Poetic Review and Friendly Offering

ISBN/EAN: 9783337416478

Printed in Europe, USA, Canada, Australia, Japan

Cover: Foto ©Andreas Hilbeck / pixelio.de

More available books at **www.hansebooks.com**

A BEAUTIFUL

POETIC REVIEW

AND

FRIENDLY OFFERING

BY

J. R. BRADWAY, M. D.,

ORATOR OF OAKLAND COUNCIL, NO. 192,

AMERICAN LEGION OF HONOR.

———

ISSUED BY

DEWEY & CO., Publishers,

SAN FRANCISCO, CAL.

1885.

PUBLISHERS' NOTE.

— —

The following graceful review, which the author has modestly alluded to as "poetical ramblings," was prepared and read in parts, at different times, by Dr. Bradway, for entertaining the fraternal council meetings in the line of his official duties therein. His hearers were so delighted as to unanimously request the publication of the papers that had, from evening to evening, fully captivated their appreciation.

The publisher, being one of the favored listeners, volunteered to issue the series in fitting style, in the faith that the little work would meet with decided favor as a pleasing literary keepsake—a convenient "catch up," as it were, for easy reading in spare moments, likely to be rarely and popularly relished.

I.

Poetry is the language of Nature. It is written in unmistakable characters all over the broad pages of her great book, and may be read and understood by all who have eyes to see, ears to hear, and minds to appreciate the sublime, the melodious and the beautiful. Natural poetry in its broadest sense includes motion, sound, color and form. The graceful waving of willow boughs in the gentle wind, the gambols of the young of animals as they skip and play in the very joy of young existence, the graceful movements of many birds in their easy flight through the ocean of air, and the fleecy summer cloud as it floats like a pure spirit over mountain and moor impelled by the summer breeze, are all familiar examples of nature's poetry of motion. The song of birds, the hum of insects, the babbling of brooks as they wind their way over pebbly bottoms, or "slip down among moss-grown stones with endless laughter;" the murmur of woodland streams, the sighing of the summer zephyr through forest and grove; the roar of the cataract and the wild chorus of the storm, are examples of the poetry of sound in the great auditorium of Nature. The flowers that deck the hillside and beautify the valley, that are spread abroad everywhere in such wild profusion over the broad lap of mother earth, are familiar examples of nature's poetry of form and color. In truth

> "The world is full of poetry—the air
> Is living with its spirits; and the waves
> Dance to the music of its melodies,
> And sparkle in its brightness. Earth is veiled

And mantled with its beauty; and the walls
That close the universe with crystal in,
Are eloquent with voices that proclaim
The unseen glories of immensity
In harmonies too perfect and too high
For aught but things of celestial mould;
And speak to man in one eternal hymn
Unfading beauty and unyielding power.
Poetry is itself a thing of God;
He made his prophets poets, and the more
We feel of poesy do we become
Like God in love and power."

II.

It has been truly said, that whatever excites the imagination, pleases the fancy, elevates, purifies, refines and ennobles our being, whether in the world of mind or matter, has in it the elements of, and comes legitimately in the dominion of poetry. Three essential poetical sentiments exist in man: The love of God, the love of woman and the love of country; the religious, the human and the political sentiment. For this reason wherever the knowledge of God is darkened, wherever the face of woman is veiled, wherever the people are led captive or enslaved, there poetry is like a flame which for want of fuel exhausts and dies out. On the contrary, wherever God reigns upon his throne in all the majesty of his glory, wherever woman rules by the irresistible power of her purity, her virtue and her enchantments, wherever the people are free, there poetry has modest roses for the woman, glorious palms for the people, and splendid wings with which to mount up to the loftiest regions of heaven. Baseness, impurity, wrong and injustice give no inspiration, produce no poets and no poetry. It has been well said, that "Poets are born, not made." Dame Nature has never granted a franchise for the manufacture of poets: has never imparted the grand secret of her power to any human institution. Education never produced a poet. It may, and does, add some bright feathers to his plumage, steadiness and strength to his flight of imagination, polish and fullness to his expression: but the beauty and sublimity of thought, the original power and vividness of imagination, the readiness of comparison, and all that constitutes the very soul must spring from that superior and peculiar cast of mind generally denominated genius.

Education, however well directed and skillful, could no more produce a poet from a common mind than Canova or Praxiteles could carve a Greek slave or a Venus de Medici from a block of pumice-stone. As well might the clumsy and unwieldy dodo attempt the flight of the strong swift-winged eagle as for the common mind to attempt the flight of genius in the sublime regions of poesy. An able teacher whose excellent instructions I once had the good fortune to enjoy, a profound mathematician, an accurate scientist, and a man of most excellent practical sense, was in the habit of lecturing his class about once a quarter on writing poetry. He was generally incited to this by discovering among the class that tendency, very common among young men of a certain age, to court the Muses, mount Pegasus and attempt to ascend the rugged heights of Helicon from whose classic summit springs the gushing fountains of poesy.

He was accustomed to say, "There are two things, young gentlemen, I would advise you never to attempt unless nature has endowed you with a special gift, viz., wit and poetry; for of all failures a failure in an attempt at wit is humiliating enough, but at poetry is still more so. Do not attempt poetry unless you can think poetry, dream poetry and talk poetry; unless it comes to you as it were by inspiration." He once related an anecdote illustrative of the ludicrous absurdity of an attempt at poetry where there is no natural gift.

A school-mate of his in his college days had become infatuated with the idea that he could write poetry. And being an aspiring young man he could not be satisfied with anything of the common order; it must reach the sublime. So with pen and paper duly arrayed, and after much abstract thought, he commenced thus:

> "The sun from his perpendicular height
> Shines into the depths of the sea—"

And here his muse halted and folded her wings. This, though, was so far quite satisfactory. It was sublime, it reached the sun; it was deep, it went down into the sea—but it was incomplete, it must be finished. So after a long and fruitless effort, feeling that his muse had deserted him, and that he could produce nothing that would properly complete the stanza, he walked forth into the fields and groves to court inspiration, hoping by his return that his muse might have so plumed her pinions as to be ready to continue her flight. During his absence his room-mate came in, and seeing the unfinished production, and knowing his friend's penchant for writing poetry, took up the pen and completed the stanza, when it read thus:

> "The sun from his perpendicular height
> Shines into the depths of the sea,
> And the fishes begin to sweat
> And cry, why d—— it, how hot we be!"

This finished the young man's efforts at poetry.

III.

Plodding and toilsome, effort alone never produce true poetry. It must rise as spontaneously from the mind as perfume from the flower, or warmth and light from the sunbeam. The Muses are not of the laboring class, and Pegasus, their steed, was endowed by the gods with winged feet that he might soar to the lofty heights of Helicon and not toil up through the dust of earth.

I think it may be asserted without the fear of successful contradiction, that no one ever rose to distinction as a poet who did not in early life give unmistakable evidence of possessing the divine gift. Milton distinguished himself as a poet before he was 16, and while yet in his teens stood at the head of English scholars as a writer of Latin verses. Pope wrote his "Pastorals" at the age of 16. Burns, though the son of a gardener and without the advantages of a liberal education, early acquired a reputation as a poet.

Byron wrote his "English Bards and Scotch Reviewers" before his majority, in answer to some criticisms by the Edinburgh *Review* on a collection of poems which he had previously written, and his "Childe Harolde" was published before he was 25. Campbell wrote early, and produced his "Pleasures of Hope," an admirable poem, which gave him instant fame as a poet, before he was 22.

Bryant, our own beloved and revered bard, who has written some of the most beautiful effusions ever written in the English language, commenced writing at 12, and produced his "Thanatopsis," a poem that has been read and admired wherever the English language is spoken, before he was 19.

Lucretia Maria Davidson, the child of song, the sweet poetical bud of promise, who drooped and died "like the early flower nipped by the unfeeling frost, just as it rose lovely in youth and put its beauties on," composed beautifully at four years of age; and though she died at 17, had produced many effusions remarkable for sweetness and beauty, showing also sublimity of thought. A quotation from one of which I cannot refrain from giving here:

> "Why these restless 'vain desires
> That constant strive for something more
> To feed the spirit's hidden fires
> That burn unseen, unnoticed soar?
> Well might the heathen sage have known
> That earth must fail the soul to bind,
> That life and life's tame joys alone
> Can never chain the ethereal mind."

It must be conceded that this is replete with the true spirit of poesy, and could not have been produced by one so young, save by inspiration of true genius. The sister, Margaret, who died somewhat younger, was equally gifted. The immortal spirit panting for its heavenly home could not be imprisoned by the frail earthly tenement by which it was enshrouded. Many more examples might be given, but what has been produced is, I think, sufficient to establish beyond a doubt that true poetry is of divine and not of earthly origin.

IV.

Having spoken of poetry in a broad and general sense, and referred briefly to some of the essential characteristics of poetry and poets, I now propose to speak more definitely of the poetry of language or written poetry. In doing which I shall call attention to three varieties of composition, viz., prose, blank verse and rhyme—the last of which is generally considered the style of composition especially entitled to the name of poetry.

As I have before stated, beauty, truth, sublimity, ideality and comparison constitute the essential elements and soul of poetry. Rhyme and meter are only characteristics in the garb which poetry generally wears, and without some of the essential elements which I have mentioned, no more constitute true poetry than form and clothing would constitute a true man. An effigy may have the form and garb of manhood and dissemble well the general appearance, but lacking vitality and soul is only a despicable, hollow sham. So composition may have the form and semblance of poetry, but without the essential elements which constitute soul it is mere jingle—an empty sham. I propose first to call attention briefly to what may be properly termed the poetry of prose. As we sometimes find the highest type of noble manhood clothed in the coarsest, simplest garb, so we often find the . very essence and soul of poetry clothed in the humble, plain garb of prose, a few examples of which, by way of illustration, I now propose to give:

The notorious Scotchman, Rob Roy, having incurred the displeasure of the constituted authorities by some grave offense against the law—which was greatly magnified by his enemies—was urged by his personal friends, who were fearful he might come to grief, to leave the country; but to all their entreaties he replied emphatically, No. Said he, "Should I do so, the very stones would cry out against me. The heather upon which I have trod while living shall bloom over my grave when I am dead." Unflinching patriotism and love of home and an unshaken determination to sleep beneath the flowers whose beauty and fragrance had charmed him while living could hardly have been expressed in language more truly poetical.

V.

The Highlanders of Scotland are deeply imbued with sentiments of poetry and romance. The rugged mountains, the romantic glens and beautiful lakes set like mirrors amid their mountain fastnesses, and the general wildness of the scenery, give a charm to their bold, free life well calculated to inspire sentiments of patriotism, poetry and romance. In like manner with the North American Indian. There is something in the solitary grandeur of the forest and the almost boundless expanse of the plains where he is accustomed to roam—in his intimate communion with nature in all the wild grandeur and boundless beauty of her primitive state, well calculated to fill the mind—all uncultured though it may be—with sentiments of poetry and romance. Hence, we often find among specimens of Indian oratory examples of lofty and sublime poetry. Red Jacket, the once famous chief of the Senecas, and one of the most distinguished of Indian orators, when passing through the State of New York—once the home and now the resting-place of his fathers—when very old was repeatedly urged to give a specimen of his oratorical powers; but feeling that age and the fire-water of the white man had greatly dimmed the brightness of those intellectual fires that once burned with such brilliancy, could not be prevailed on to attempt a speech. For this unwillingness he on one occasion offered the following remarkable apology: Rising in his place with something like the native grandeur and dignity of former years (for he still retained much of physical vigor), he said, "I am an aged hemlock. The winds of nearly a hundred winters have blown through my branches, and I am dead at the top." What language could express more poetically that period in man's life when the fire of genius burns low, when the brilliant intellect has fallen into the sere and yellow leaf while the physical powers are yet comparatively vigorous ? Any one acquainted with the forests of our middle and northern States, who has seen the sturdy hemlock with its dry and leafless crown, while all below was green and vigorous, will readily perceive the striking beauty and truthfulness of the illustration used.

VI.

But no man, perhaps, who has written in the English language, has interwoven more of the beauty and true sentiment of poetry in his prose writings than our own much-loved and respected countryman, Washington Irving. There is about his writings a clearness of style, a beauty and simplicity of language, a purity of sentiment and expression, a truthfulness and vividness of illustration that constitutes the very soul and essence of poetry, a few examples of which I will here present. From his sketch entitled "The Wife," we have the following: "As the vine which has long twined its graceful foliage about the oak and been lifted by it into sunshine, will, when the hardy plant is rifted by the thunderbolt, cling round it with its caressing tendrils and bind up its shattered boughs, so is it beautifully ordered by Providence that woman, who is the mere dependent and ornament of man in his happier hours, should be his stay and solace when smitten by sudden calamity; winding herself into the rugged recesses of his nature, tenderly supporting his drooping head, and binding up the broken heart." Again from the sketch entitled the "Broken Heart:" "How many bright eyes grow dim, how many soft cheeks grow pale, how many lovely forms fade away into the tomb, and none can tell the cause that blighted their loveliness! As the dove will clasp its wings to its side and cover and conceal the arrow that is preying upon its vitals, so it is the nature of woman to hide from the world the pangs of wounded affection. * * * She is like some tender tree, the pride and beauty of the grove; graceful in its form, bright in its foliage, but with the worm preying at its heart. We find it suddenly withering when it should be most fresh and luxuriant. We see it drooping its branches to the earth, and shedding leaf by leaf, until, wasted and perished away it falls, even in the stillness of the forest, and as we muse over the beautiful ruin we strive in vain to recollect the blast or thunderbolt that could have smitten it with decay."

It was of this sketch, "The Broken Heart," that Byron once said he "wanted to hear an American read it," and when an American read it to him he melted into tears, remarking, "You see me weep; I have but few tears for this world, but I always weep for the broken heart, and I do not believe Irving ever wrote that piece without weeping." The following from his "Traits of Indian Character" is full of poetical beauty: "But if courage intrinsically consists in the defiance of danger and pain, the life of the Indian is a continual exhibition of it. * * * As the ship careers in fearful single-ness through the solitudes of ocean; as the bird mingles among clouds and storms and wings its way, a mere speck, across the pathless fields of air, so the Indian holds his course—silent, solitary, but undaunted, through the bound-less bosom of the wilderness. * * * He gains his food by the hardships and dangers of the chase; he wraps himself in the spoils of the bear, the panther and the buffalo, and sleeps among the thunders of the cataract."

I find so many passages of exquisite beauty and so replete with poetical sentiment in perusing the writings of this author that I scarcely know where to stop. What I have given, however, I deem sufficient to illustrate the idea presented and to show the character of the composition which I have thought proper to denominate the poetry of prose. There is, however, one other author whose prose writing contains so much of real poetic sentiment and exquisite beauty that I cannot refrain from introducing to your notice one quotation. The author is the late G. D. Prentice, formerly of the Louisville *Journal*, and the extract is from a piece of rare beauty of style and language, which he wrote many years since, entitled "The Thunder Storm:" "My dread of, thunder had its origin in an incident that occurred when I was a boy of ten years. I had a cousin, a girl of the same age of myself, who had been the constant companion of my childhood. Strange that after the lapse of so many years that countenance should be so familiar to me. I can see the bright young creature, her eyes flashing like a beautiful gem, her free locks streaming as with joy upon the rising gale, her cheek glowing like a ruby through transparent snow. Her voice had the melody and joyousness of a bird's, and when she bounded over the woodland hill, or fresh green valley, shouting a glad answer to every voice of nature, and clapping her little hands in the very ecstasy of young existence, she looked as if breaking away, a free nightingale, from earth, and going off where all things are beautiful and happy like her." The whole piece is a gem in prose composition of rare beauty, but this must suffice.

VII.

Having dwelt sufficiently upon what I have denominated the poetry of prose, I now propose to call attention to that style of poetical composition called blank verse, which differs from the poetry of prose, principally, in adding what may be fitly denominated an element of form, viz., meter, giving to each line a certain number of accented syllables. Blank verse, containing thus one more element of finished poetry, may be considered the higher order of composition, and therefore better adapted to the expression of the grand, the beautiful and the sublime in thought and action. It is the style of composition seldom or never attempted by the tyro and the uncultivated, but belongs especially to the cultured and the scholastic. Milton's "Paradise Lost" and Pollock's "Course of Time" are familiar and excellent examples of this style of poetical composition, abounding in sublimity of thought, and beauty and force of

expression—a few examples of which I will here give by way of illustration.
Eve, upon leaving Paradise, thus gives expression to her grief:

> " O unexpected stroke, worse than of death !
> Must I leave thee, Paradise? thus leave
> Thee, native soil, these happy walks and shades
> Fit haunt of gods? where I had hoped to spend,
> Quiet though sad, the respite of that day
> That must be mortal to us both."

It would seem that no other style of composition could so forcibly express
the deep, impassioned grief of Eve on her departure from Paradise. The following quotation from Pollock will illustrate the descriptive power of this
style of composition:

> " He touched his harp and nations heard entranced.
> As some vast river of unfailing source,
> Rapid, exhaustless, deep, his numbers flowed,
> And opened new fountains in the human heart;
> Where fancy halted, weary in its flight
> In other men, his, fresh as morning rose,
> And soared untrodden heights, and seemed at home
> Where angels bashful looked. Others, though great,
> Beneath their argument seemed struggling while
> He from above descending stooped to touch
> The loftiest thought; and proudly stooped, as though
> It scarce deserved his verse. With Nature's self
> He seemed an old acquaintance, free to jest
> At will with all her glorious majesty."

A more grand and complete description could scarcely be given of a great poet than this. Another quotation, quite different in character, will show the power of this style of composition for varied expression and vivid delineation:

> "'Twas pitiful to see the early flower
> Nipped by the unfeeling frost, just as it rose
> Lovely in youth and put its beauties on."

This is full of tender sympathy and exquisite beauty. Again:

> "Sad was the sight of widowed, childless age,
> Weeping. I saw it once. Wrinkled with time,
> And hoary with the dust of years, an old
> And worthy man came to his humble roof.
> His lonely cot was silent, and he looked
> As if he could not enter. On his staff,
> Bending, he leaned, and from his weary eye—
> Distressing sight! a single tear-drop wept.
> None followed, for the fount of tears was dry.
> Alone and last, it fell from wrinkle down
> To wrinkle, till it lost itself: drunk by
> The withered cheek on which again no smile
> Would come or drop of tenderness be seen."

It would, I think, be difficult to conceive of a picture of deeper woe and more utter desolation than the one the poet has here given. For further illustration I shall quote briefly from the writings of the late George D. Prentice, formerly of the Louisville *Journal*, whose imagination and pen have given us some productions not excelled by any other writer in the English language. In a poem of his, entitled "The Closing Year," we find the following:

" 'Tis midnight's holy hour—and silence now
Is brooding like a gentle spirit o'er
The still and pulseless world.   Hark! On the winds
The bell's deep tones are swelling; 'tis the knell
Of the departed year.   No funeral train
Is sweeping past, yet, on the stream and wood,
With melancholy light, the moonbeams re st
Like a pale, spotless shroud; the air is stirred
As by a mourner's sigh; and on yon cloud
That floats so still and placidly through heaven,
The spirits of the seasons seem to stand.
Young Spring, bright Summer, Autumn's solemn form
And Winter with his aged locks, and breathe
In mournful cadences, that come abroad
Like the far wind-harp's wild and touching wail,
A melancholy dirge o'er the dead year
Gone from the earth forever.   'Tis a time
For memory and for tears."

This is replete with beauty, pathos, and solemn sublimity. Another quotation from the same author, somewhat different in sentiment, will not, I presume, be uninteresting. It is from a piece entitled "The Stars." Thus:

" Those burning stars! What are they? I have dreamed
That they were blossoms on the tree of life,
Or glory flung back from the outspread wings
Of God's archangels—or that yon blue sky,
With all its gorgeous blazonry of gems,
Were but a banner waving o'er the earth
From the far wall of heaven; and I have sat
And drank their gushing glory till I felt
Their flash electric trembling with deep

And strong vibrations down the living wire
Of chainless passion—and my very pulse
Was beating high, as if a spring were there
To buoy me up where I might ever roam
'Mid the unfathomed vastness of the sky,
And dwell with those high stars, and see their light
Poured down upon the blessed earth like dew
From the bright wings of naiads."

This is full of beautiful imagery, touching pathos, and unmeasured sublimity. It would be difficult to conceive anything more beautiful in language, more lofty in thought. The poet's muse seems to soar on outspread wing among the distant stars. This I deem sufficient to illustrate the power and adaptability of this style of composition to the expression of the beautiful in thought, action, and emotion.

VIII.

I now pass to the consideration of that style of poetical composition which, in addition to the poetical elements heretofore considered, adds that of rhyme, which is considered by many readers the crowning element in poetical composition. It does indeed give a charm to poetical composition not otherwise attainable; but it is only an element of form, and is to poetry what exquisite finish is to statuary—it rounds and softens, adding beauty of finish to grandeur of outline. Blank verse may be said to possess more rugged grandeur; rhyme more finished beauty. Perhaps I cannot better illustrate the difference than by giving the following quotations, in the different styles of composition, on the same subject:

"Oh, Winter! ruler of the inverted year,
Thy scattered hair with sleet-like ashes fill'd,

> Thy breath congeal'd upon thy lips, thy cheeks
> Fringed with a beard made white with other snows
> Than those of age; thy forehead wrapped in clouds,
> A leafless branch thy scepter, and thy throne
> A sliding car indebted to no wheels
> But urged by storms along its slipp'ry way—
> I love thee, all unlovely as thou seem'st,
> And dreaded as thou art."

Again:

> " Gently as lilies shed their leaves
> When Summer's days are fair,
> The feath'ry snow comes floating down,
> Like blossoms on the air;
> And o'er the world like angels' wings,
> Unfolding soft and white,
> It broods above the brown sear earth
> And fills with forms of light
> The dead and desolate domain,
> Where Winter holds his iron reign."

Though both styles of composition are susceptible of great variations, yet the above illustration will give a tolerable idea of the difference in expression. And here I would remark that in the consideration of written poetry, for the purpose of illustration, I have thought proper to divide its elements into two classes. The first I would denominate the soul or essential essence; the second, the form and features, in some instances only the garb it wears. The first comprises imagination, ideality, sublimity, comparison, truth, purity and beauty; the second class comprises rhythm and meter in their several varieties. The highest quality of all these elements united constitutes the most perfect type of poetical composition. But it is not necessary that every specimen of poetry that claims rank as genuine should contain all the elements above-mentioned, but sufficient of the first class to constitute soul that is easily recognized, and of the second to give comeliness of form and features. Indeed it is possible to have the soul without the form and features, as, in the poetry of prose; but the reverse is hardly possible, for rhythm and meter, however perfect, without some element of the first class could be little else than mere doggerel or senseless jingle. Genuine poetry must have soul.

IX.

There is no element in poetical composition so abused and actually murdered by the ignorant and presumptuous as the element of rhyme. Persons who would not attempt to write a sentence in plain prose, will, under the inspiration of some unusual occasion, write what *they* term poetry, but which is in reality the most nonsensical jingle, coming about as near the genuine article as the rattling of marbles in a tin can comes to genuine music.

I very well remember, many years ago, when but an idle boy, it was customary for the peddlers of small wares and Yankee notions, to hawk about the streets what were called "ballads," a rhythmical detail of some remarkable incident, an accident accompanied with loss of life, a murder, an execution, or some incident with harrowing details. A couple of stanzas of one of these productions I still remember. It has clung to my memory through the many years that have since gone by on the wings of light and shadow. The inspiring incident was as follows: A party of young people, in the buoyancy of youth, were out enjoying a sleigh ride, when crossing a stream the ice gave way and all were drowned. The stanzas ran as follows:

> " Schoharrie stream they sought to cross,
>   Not knowing they would suffer loss;
>   The ice gave way and down they went,
>   And thus their life and breath was spent.
>   Under the ice they all did go,
>   Which caused their friends the deepest woe;
>   And several anxious days rolled round,
>   Before their bodies could be found.

The ballad continued, describing the funeral, the grief of the friends and neighbors, and enumerated the virtues of the departed, but I will not attempt to give any more, as it has so nearly faded from my memory that I could not do it justice.

But this class of poets and this style of poetry is so admirably taken off in what is known as the "Bedott Papers," that I am sure I cannot do better than quote from them by way of illustration.

It will be remembered that Mrs. Bedott was one of those home-made, self-constituted poets who feel inspired to write upon every important incident that happens in the family or neighborhood. It is generally occasions of grief or misfortune that stirs up the muse of this class of poets. Thus, on the death of neighbor Bennett, Mrs. Bedott wrote the following "consolin'" varses to his afflicted widder."

> " O Gandefield,
>   Where is thy shield
>   To guard against grim death ?
>   He aims his gun
>   At old and young,
>   And fires away their breath.

" One summer's day
    For to tend to his hay
Mr. Bennett went to the medder,
    Fell down from the stack,
    Broke the spine of his back,
And left a mournin' widder.

" 'Twas occasioned by his landin'
    On a jug that was standin'
        Alongside of the stack of hay.
Some folks say 'twas *what was in it*
Caused the fall of Mr. Bennett,
    But there aint a word of truth in what they say."

On another occasion, hearing that Elder Sniffles, a lone widower to whom she was becoming very partial, was sick, she writes as follows by way of consolation :

" O Reverend Sir, I do declare,
    It drives me al'most to frenzy
To think o' you a lyin' there
    Down sick with influenzy.

" O, I could to your bedside fly
    And wipe your weepin' eyes,
And try my best to cure you up,
    If it wouldn't create surprise."

But Elder Sniffles recovered, and the old lady's interest in him increased so much that 'twas *love* and not sympathy that inspired her muse when she wrote as follows :

> " Ere love had teached my tears to flow
> I was oncommon cheerful,
> But now such misery I do know,
> I'm always sad and fearful.
>
> " Full forty dollars would I give
> If we had contincred apart,
> For though he's made my sperit live,
> He's surely bust my heart."

But fortunately for the lovers of poetry the old lady did not die of a "busted heart," but lived to become a happy, blushing bride, and in the exu berance of her joy to enrich the world of literature with the following from her gifted pen, addressed to her "fortinit" husband, Shadrack :

> " 'O, Shadrack, *my* Shadrack !' Priscilla did speak,
> While the rosy red blushes surmantled her cheek,
> And the tears of affection bedazzled her eye,
> 'O, Shadrack, my Shadrack ! I'm yourn till I die.
> The heart that was scornful and cold as a stun
> Has surrendered at last to the fortinit one.
> Farewell to the miseries and griefs I've had,
> I'll never desert thee, O Shadrack, my Shad !' "

After enjoying the sweets of second-hand matrimony for a season, with the fire of inspiration still burning brightly in her loyal "buzum," and her muse yet poised on half-closed wings, she gives vent to the following :

> " Blest be the day of sacred mirth
> That gave my dear companion birth ;   ·
> Let men rejoice while Silly sings
> The bliss her precious Shadrack brings."

X.

There is yet another variety of this class of poetry to which I wish to call attention that is not inaptly sometimes called " graveyard poetry," from the fact that it is generally found on tombstones. It is generally the effusion of some affectionate, friend who, inspired by the occasion, gives expression to some tender sentiment or commemorates some virtue possessed by the dear one now resting quietly beneath the daisies ; or perhaps personates that dear one, leaving some words of advice or consolation to the dear bereaved ones left behind, as the following:

> " Fond parents weep for me no more
> That I no more am given;
> We'll surely meet when life is o'er,
> High up above in heaven."

Or it may be an ante-mortem production of the one whose virtues and tribulations it commemorates, as the following from the pen of Mrs. Bedott. When her matters with the elder were in rather a doubtful state, and her mind harrowed by the torments of uncertainty, and feeling sure that she could not long survive the withering. blighting effect of disappointment, and that she might have everything in readiness, she wrote the following for her tombstone:

> " Here sleeps Priscilly P. Bedott,
> Late relic of Hezekier;
> How melancholy was her lot !
> How soon she did expire !
> She didn't commit self-suicide,
> 'Twas tribbilation killed her;
> O, what a pity she hadn't a-died,
> Afore she met the elder."

Or it may be a simple statement as to whom the deceased was, and what happened to him, and always, of course, in rhyme, as the following:

> " Here lies John Shaw,
>   Attorney-at-law;
>   When he died
>   The devil cried,
>   'Give us your paw,
>   John Shaw, attorney-at-law.' "

This is sufficient for illustration. I have dwelt somewhat upon this kind of poetry because there is so much of it afloat—mere trash—no more like the genuine article than the ragged cast-off garments of a man stuffed with straw and surmounted by a pasteboard mask or a carved pumpkin is like the real living, breathing man.

XI.

I wish now to call attention to that kind of poetical composition, each specimen of which, possessing more or less of the genuine elements of poetry, in a fair degree of perfection, is entitled to rank as the genuine article. I have heretofore remarked that every specimen of genuine poetry need not necessarily contain all the elements I have enumerated, but sufficient of the first class to give soul, and of the second class to give comeliness of form and features. For example, Longfellow's "Psalm of Life:"

> " Tell me not in mournful numbers,
>   Life is but an empty dream;
>   For the soul is dead that slumbers,
>   And things are not what they seem.

"Life is real, life is earnest,
   And the grave is not its goal;
Dust thou art, to dust returnest,
   Was not spoken of the soul."

Here we have but a shadow of ideality, combined with a pure and lofty sentiment, and with sublime truth beautifully and forcibly spoken. The rhythm and meter are perfect, each word seeming to drop gently into its place without study or effort—no transposition or distortion to produce measure or meter, but an easy flow of language like the musical murmur of a gentle stream. The following also from the pen of our own revered Bryant, as plain descriptive poetry is equally perfect and beautiful in its way:

"Chained in the market-place he stood,
   A man of giant frame,
Amid the gathering multitude,
   That shrunk to hear his name.

"All stern of look and strong of limb,
   His dark eye on the ground,
And silently they gazed on him
   As on a lion bound."

Here, as in the former example, there is no apparent effort to produce rhyme or meter, and yet each is perfect, presenting the subject in a manner clear and forcible, and in language plain, yet beautiful.

Equal in meter and rhyme, but superior in the higher elements, is the following from the immortal Burns, occurring in his inimitable poem, "Tam O'Shanter":

"Pleasures are like poppies spread,
You seize the flower, its bloom is shed;
Or like the snowflake on the river,
A moment white, then gone forever.

"Or like the borealis race,
That flits ere you can point the place;
Or like the rainbow's lovely form,
Evanishing amidst the storm."

Here we have beauty of language, ideality, sublimity of thought illustrated by truthful comparison. Any one who has plucked a full-blown poppy, and with regret seen its bright petals fall ere he had severed it from the parent stem, or stood on the bank of a smoothly gliding stream and watched the feathery snowflakes as they fell lightly on its dark bosom, or watched the constant and rapid changes of the aurora borealis, or the sudden disappearance of the rainbow, will be convinced of the beauty and truth of the poet's illustrations.

Also the following from the pen of our revered Bryant, as he gazes upon the frail form and wan, wasted features of a dying girl—a victim of consumption:

"Death should come
Gently and to one of gentle mould like thee,
As light winds wandering through groves of bloom
Detach the delicate blossoms from the tree."

This is full of beauty, ideality touching pathos, exquisite tenderness, and truthful illustration. Any one who has walked among blooming trees and seen their delicate blossoms showered down by the gently passing breeze, will appreciate the truth, beauty and appropriateness of the poet's illustration.

And again, from the gifted pen of Miss Landon, on the same subject, we have the following:

"Day by day,
The gentle creature died away,
As parts the odor from the rose—
As fades the sky at twilight's close—
She passed, so tender and so fair."

We can scarcely conceive of anything in language more exquisitely beautiful and highly figurative.

XII.

In the above quotations we have examples of what I regard as the highest type of poetry, possessing all the essential elements. This type and style of poetry may be said to bear the same relation to plain prose that the artistically finished painting, with all of its beauty of coloring and minuteness of detail, does to the plain pencil sketch.

There is perhaps no better illustration of this than we find in the familiar piece, from the pen of Byron, entitled "The Destruction of Sennecharib."

Sennecharib, King of Assyria, having ravaged portions of Judea and laid waste many of her large cities, determined upon the destruction of Jerusalem, the great and beautiful city of Judea. To this end he encompassed it with a mighty army. Hezekiah, king of Judea, feeling unable to resist so formidable an enemy, and being greatly in fear that the city would be destroyed, appealed earnestly to the God of Israel for divine guidance and protection. The Lord of Hosts answered him through the mouth of his prophet, Hosea, saying, "The Assyrian shall not injure the chosen city, nor enter its gates; he shall not build a bank against it nor even shoot an arrow into it, but shall return the way he came to his own country." And so it came to pass, for 185,000 of

his army perished in one night. After which Sennecharib, gathering together
the remnant, returned the way he came, as the prophet had foretold.

This is the plain statement of history, which we will now compare with
the poetical description as given by Byron, that prince of poets:

"The Assyrian came down like a wolf on the fold,
And his cohorts were gleaming with purple and gold;
And the sheen of their spears was like stars on the sea,
When the deep waves roll nightly on deep Galilee.

"Like the leaves of the forest when summer is green,
That host with their banners at sunset were seen;
Like the leaves of the forest when autumn hath blown,
That host on the morrow lay withered and strewn.

"For the Angel of Death spread his wings on the blast,
And breathed in the face of the foe as he passed;
And the eyes of the sleeper waxed deadly and chill,
And their hearts but once heaved, and forever were still.

"And there lay the steed, with his nostrils all wide,
But through them rolled not the breath of his pride,
And the foam of his gasping lay white on the turf,
And cold as the spray on the rock-beaten surf.

"And there lay the rider, distorted and pale,
With the dew on his brow and the rust on his mail;
And the tents were all silent, the banners alone,
The lances unlifted, the trumpet unblown.

"And the widows of Asher are loud in their wail,
And the idols are broke in the temple of Baal;
And the might of the Gentile, unsmote by the sword,
Hath melted like snow in the glance of the Lord."

What could more forcibly illustrate the cruel rapacity of a conqueror who seeks only conquest and rapine, than a wolf, gaunt with hunger, with jaws distended and eyes gleaming with the fire of cruelty, descending upon the helpless fold, thirsty for the blood of its victims? But let us contemplate briefly the picture which the poet has spread out before us. In imagination we stand upon the walls of Jerusalem, and what do we behold? A mighty host, an army with banners, chariots and horsemen, extending in every direction as far as the eye can reach; and, as the sun sinks to the horizon, his last rays are glinted back by spear and helmet, by saber and shield and battle-axe. What could more fitly represent the almost countless host than "the leaves of the forest when summer is green," and what more vividly represent the miraculous change in this mighty host, which the morrow's sun revealed, than "the leaves of the forest when autumn hath blown"—the faded and withered leaves of the forest when the blighting frost and the fierce winds of autumn have sent them dry and withered to the ground? Where a few short hours before was the stir and bustle of a mighty army settling down to rest, now reigns the stillness and desolation of death—

> "The tents are all silent, the banners alone,
> The lances unlifted, the trumpet unblown."

And what, we are led to ask, has produced this mighty change?

> "The Angel of Death spread his wings on the blast,
> And breathed in the face of the foe as he passed;
> And the eyes of the sleepers waxed deadly and chill,
> And the hearts but once heaved, and forever were still."

What more striking illustration of the effect of a great pestilence or the fatal simoon of the desert, could be drawn than that which the poet has here given—Death spreading his dark wings over the sleeping host and breathing his withering breath in the face of each sleeper as he passed?

But let us draw nearer and examine the details of this terrible picture. We behold steeds and riders lying everywhere intermingled in dire confusion, and all in the profound stillness of death—

> "The steed with his nostrils all wide,
> But through them rolls not the breath of his pride;
> And the foam of his gasping lies white on the turf,
> And cold as the spray of the rock-beating surf.
>
> "And there lies the rider, distorted and pale,
> With the dew on his brow and the rust on his mail."

Any one who has stood upon a battle-field in the cold gray dawn of a morning succeeding a great battle must recognize the truthfulness of the picture which the poet has here drawn—a most terrible picture of a most remarkable event, which I believe has no parallel in history. 185,000 men stretched upon the plain, wrapped in that sleep that knows no waking, is a scene of which we can have no adequate conception—

> "The might of the Gentile unsmote by the sword,
> Hath melted like snow in the glance of the Lord."

XIII.

There are instances in which poetry seems the result of supernatural inspiration; when a power not of earth seems to direct the poet's thoughts and indite his words. There is perhaps no better illustration of this than that wonderfully popular production entitled "Drake's American Flag." The flag itself I have always regarded as a thing of sublime inspiration, and the poet's conception of its production is not equaled, I think, in the English language, one verse of which is as follows :

> "When Freedom from her mountain height
>   Unfurled her standard to the air,
> She tore the azure robe of night,
>   And set her stars of glory there.
> She mingled with its gorgeous dyes,
> The milky baldric of the skies,
> And striped its pure celestial white
> With streakings of the morning light;
> Then from his mansion in the sun,
> She called her eagle-bearer down,
> And gave into his mighty hand
> The symbol of her chosen land."

The poet's muse here seems not to toil laboriously up, or to poise on half-closed wings, but to spring like an eagle from his mountain crag and soar away exultingly on strong and full-spread pinions.

What more fitting source of the colors of our glorious flag, and the stars that deck its azure field like blossoms of light, than the heavens. And what more appropriate emblem of free, proud, happy, enterprising America than the clear-sighted, strong, swift-winged eagle—the bird of Jove, "Who can stem the fury of the northern blast and bathe his plumage in the thunder's home"—who is alike at home in the torrid or the frigid zone, on the mountain or in the valley, wherever the Stars and Stripes float over American soil!

There are instances when the poetic mind seems to draw superhuman inspiration from the times, the occasion and surrounding circumstances combined—when the muse seems endowed with eagle's wings, the far-seeing vision of the inspired prophet inditing truth and prophecy in "thoughts that breathe and words that burn."

There is, perhaps, no better illustration of this than that grand and beautiful effusion, by Mrs. Julia Ward Howe, the "Battle Hymn of the Republic."

It is said that Mrs. Howe had been, for some time during the first year of the Rebellion, desirous of producing something from her pen appropriate to the times and the occasion, that could be sung to the soul-stirring music of "John Brown."

On one occasion, while the national Capitol was encircled with armies, and the whole city was one grand military encampment, where the sound of martial music and the measured tramp of soldiers could be heard on every side, she was invited by a military friend to visit the encampments around the city, and witness the preparations for defence, the drill and parade of "the boys in blue." She gladly accepted the invitation, and with a heart swelling with patriot emotions, looked upon the serried ranks, the "rows of burnished steel;" witnessed the various evolutions and the drill, by which fathers, sons and brothers were being prepared for the momentous struggle in which they were soon to engage.

Remaining till after dark, she saw, with a swelling soul, the "watch-fires of a hundred circling camps," and she saw, too, the incense ascending from the altars built to Jehovah "in the evening dews and damps," and as she passed regiment after regiment, and heard, with emotions too deep for utterance, the inspiring music of "John Brown" swelling up from thousands of patriotic throats, she felt justly proud of her great country and its noble defenders. Returned to her home, her heart thrilling with that noble Christian patriotism that filled the breasts of so many of our noble American matrons, manifesting itself in their lives and deeds, she felt more than ever desirous of accomplishing the task she had contemplated. That night, when she repaired to her couch it was not to sleep. The incidents and scenes of the day were constantly before her mind.

The great wrong and injustice of human slavery, and the wrath of a just God that must, sooner or later, be visited upon its advocates and supporters, were constantly in her thoughts, till she finally arose and wrote, as by inspiration, nearly as we now have it, the following sublime effusion:

Mine eyes have seen the glory of the coming of the Lord;
He is trampling out the vintage where the grapes of wrath are stored;
He hath loosed the faithful lightning of His terrible swift sword:
    His truth is marching on.

I have seen Him in the watch-fires of a hundred circling camps;
They have builded Him an altar in the evening dews and damps;
I can see His righteous sentence in the dim and flaring lamps;
    His day is marching on.

I have read a fiery gospel writ in rows of burnished steel:
As ye deal with my contemners, so my grace with you shall deal;
Let the Hero, born of woman, crush the serpent with his heel,
    Since God is marching on.

He has sounded forth the trumpet that shall never call retreat;
He is sifting out the hearts of men before His judgment seat.

O! be swift, my soul, to answer Him! be jubilant, my feet;
    Our God is marching on.

In the beauty of the lilies Christ was born across the sea,
With a glory in his bosom that transfigures you and me;
As he died to make men holy, let us die to make men free,
    While God is marching on.

For grandeur of thought, sublimity of conception, keenness of prophetic vision, beauty and purity of language—in short, all that is necessary to constitute genuine poetry, it is not excelled by anything in the English language.

It is one of those rare poetic gems, which, like "The Star Spangled Banner, "Hail Columbia," "America," and a few others, are sure to shine in the diadem of the patriotic literature of America while she holds her place among the nations of the earth, or her sons and daughters retain a spark of that noble patriotism which is their just inheritance.

XIV.

In conclusion, I would here remark it has been my aim to give expression to my ideas—crude though they may be—of the essential elements of poetry, its nature and office, and to show by contrast the difference between genuine poetry and mere jingle or doggerel, the latter being mere nonsense or rhyme run mad, while the former, whether in the form of prose, blank verse or rhyme, is always replete with purity of thought, beauty of language, and sublimity of ideas, well calculated to arouse the nobler and more refined sentiments of man's nature.

In all ages and in all countries, poetry has nerved the soldier's arm to strike for truth and the right, and commemorated his deeds of valor; it has stimulated the patriot's zeal, the scholar's enthusiasm, and brightened the Christian's hopes.

The poetry of a people has in all ages marked their degree of civilization and refinement; and it has been truthfully said, he who writes the songs of a nation wields a controlling influence over its destiny. It is the language in which the heart's deepest, tenderest emotions are expressed, and by which its inmost fountains are stirred.

In giving expression to these crude thoughts, I have hoped to show, somewhat, the importance of cultivating in the minds of the young a taste for the study of high-toned, genuine poetry for its elevating and refining influence. If I have succeeded in the smallest degree, I shall feel amply paid for the labor and thought I have expended.

www.ingramcontent.com/pod-product-compliance
Lightning Source LLC
Chambersburg PA
CBHW030913260626
47169CB00008B/2831